YO GABBA GABBA!

IT'S NICE TO MEET YOU!

ADAPTED BY NATALIE SHAW   BASED ON THE SCREENPLAY "FAMILY" WRITTEN BY
CHRISTIAN JACOBS AND SARAH DYER

ILLUSTRATED BY MIKE GILES

SIMON SPOTLIGHT
New York   London   Toronto   Sydney

SIMON SPOTLIGHT An imprint of Simon & Schuster Children's Publishing Division 1230 Avenue of the Americas, New York, New York 10020
Based on the TV series *Yo Gabba Gabba!*™ as seen on Nick Jr.™

For information about special discounts for bulk purchases, please contact Simon & Schuster Special Sales
at 1-866-506-1949 or business@simonandschuster.com.
Manufactured in the United States of America 0711 LAK 10 9 8 7 6 5 4 ISBN 978-1-4169-9721-4

"Oh, Muno!" DJ Lance called out one afternoon. "I have a special surprise for you."

"Oh, boy! What is it?" asked Muno. "I love surprises!"

"Close your eye and you'll find out!" said DJ Lance.

"Okay, Muno. Turn around and take a look," said DJ Lance. "Surprise! Your family is in Gabba Land for a visit."

"Mom! Dad! Hey!" shouted Muno. He was so excited to see everyone!

"Muno, why don't you introduce me to your family?" DJ Lance suggested.

"Okay, let's see," Muno said. "There are one, two, three, four, five people in my family. We are best friends and we love one another!"

"This is my dad!" Muno began. "He's the first member of my family."
"Hi, I'm Muno's father," said Muno's dad. "I love computers and old
cowboy movies. Yeehaw!"

"The second member of my family is my mom," Muno continued. "Hi, I'm Muno's mother," said Muno's mom. "I love Chihuahuas and Chinese noodles."

"The third member of my family is my big sister," said Muno, proudly. "Hi. My name is Chibo," said Muno's sister. "I love school and baby owls."

"Now, Muno, who is the fourth member of our family?" asked Muno's mom.

"Oh, right! That's me!" said Muno. "My name is Muno. I love bugs and playing with my friends."

"And the fifth member of our family is our little baby, Gogo," said Muno's mom. "He loves being happy!"

"Hey, Muno," Chibo said, "I'd really like to meet all of your friends."
"I'd love to meet them too!" said Muno's mom.

Muno called to his friends. "Foofa! Brobee! Toodee! Plex! Come here, everyone."

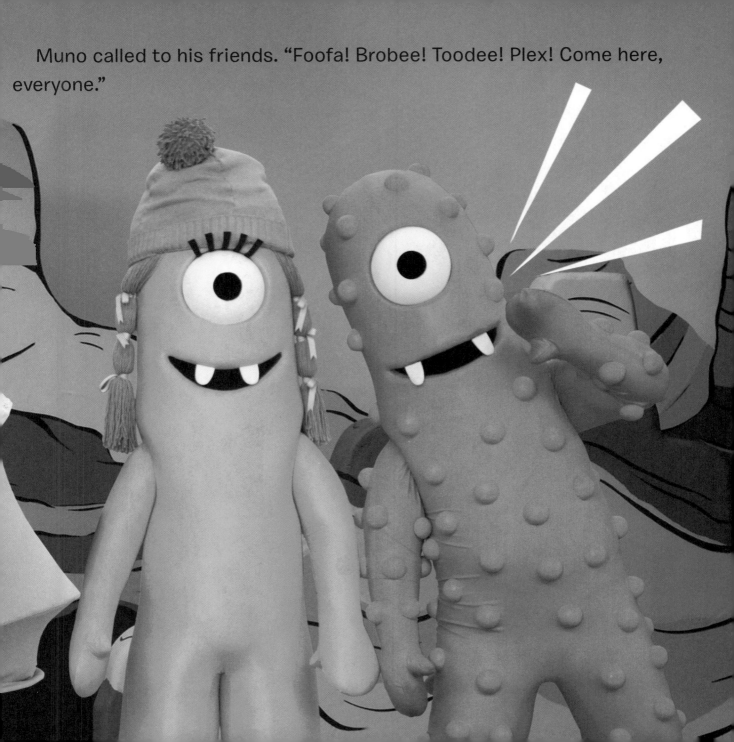

Foofa and Brobee came running out, but when they saw Muno's family, they stopped. They didn't want to come any closer.

"What's going on?" Brobee asked Muno.

"Brobee, Foofa, I want you to meet my family," said Muno.

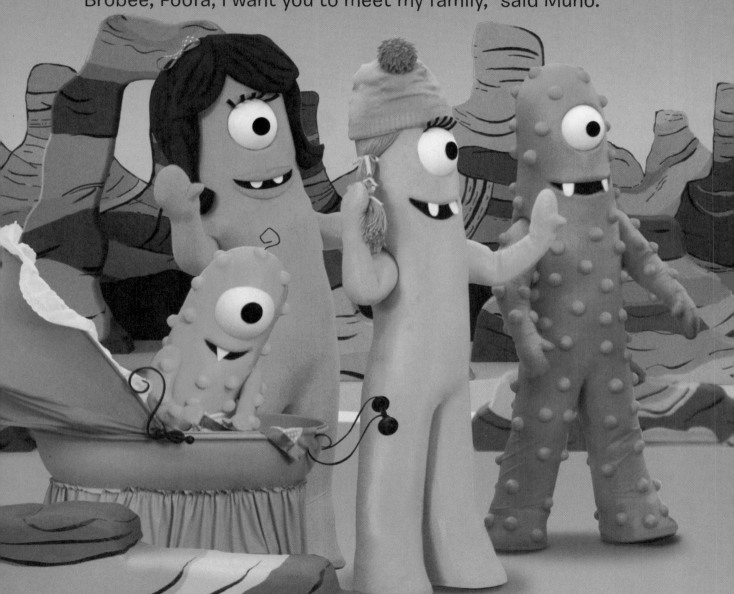

Muno's dad reached out to shake Brobee's hand. "It's nice to meet you, Brobee!" he said.

But Brobee didn't say anything, and he kept his hands behind his back.

"Don't worry, kids!" said Muno's dad. "We're as nice as boysenberry pie."

"It's really nice to meet some of Muno's friends," added Muno's mom.

But Brobee and Foofa didn't say anything.

"Hey, guys, what's wrong?" asked Muno.

Just then Plex and Toodee walked by.

"Well, hello, Muno. This must be your family," Plex said.

"Yeah!" said Muno. "I wanted them to meet everybody, but Foofa and Brobee aren't talking."

Plex thought he knew what was wrong. "Brobee and Foofa just aren't used to meeting new people," he said. "Maybe they don't know what to say."

"But these aren't new people. This is my family," said Muno.

"They're new people to Foofa and Brobee," Plex explained.
Plex turned to Brobee and Foofa. "When we meet new friends, we should tell them our names and then say, 'It's nice to meet you!' It's a great way to meet new people!"

"When I meet new friends, like Muno's family," sang Plex.
"I say my name and try to be friendly.
I say 'Hello, my name is Plex. How do you do?'"

Muno's mom joined in.
"*And then I say 'I am Muno's mom. It's nice to meet you!'*"
"*It's nice to meet you, too!*" sang Plex.

"*Hello. You must be Muno's dad.*" Plex continued singing.
"Yes, that's right," said Muno's dad, and then he started singing too.
"*When we meet new friends it's nice to say our names and 'How are you?'*
We can also shake hands and say, 'It's so nice to meet you.'"

"Hi, everybody!" said Chibo.
"I'm Muno's sister and this is Gogo."
"Hey! My name is Toodee," said
Toodee. "It's nice to meet you!"

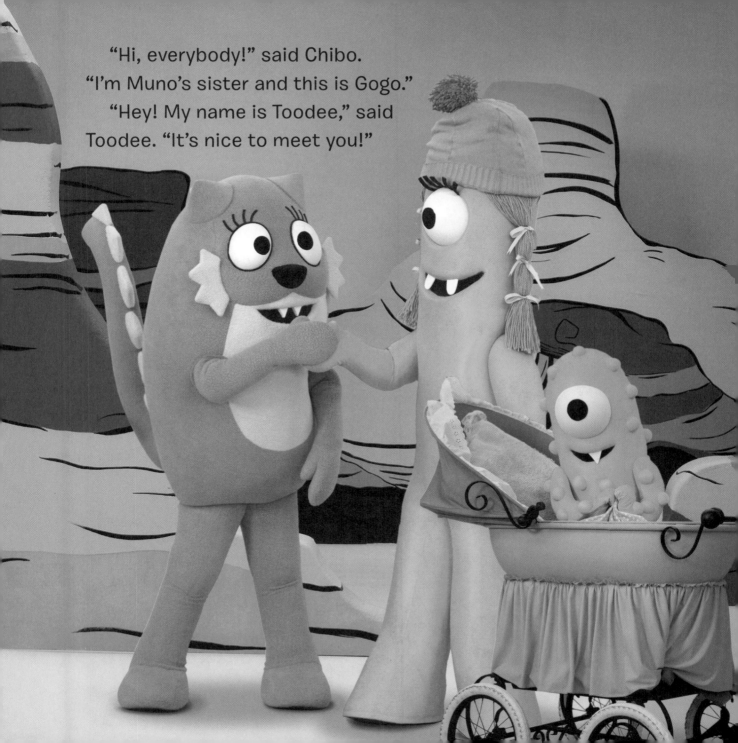

"Now I understand," said Foofa. "Hi, everyone. I'm Foofa. It's nice to meet you!"

"And I'm Brobee," Brobee said. "It's nice to meet you too!"

"It's nice to meet you, Brobee and Foofa!" said Muno's family.

"Hi, Foofa!" said Chibo.
"It's nice to meet you, Chibo!" said Foofa. "Would you like to play with us?"
"Yeah!" said Chibo. "Let's go!"

The Gabba gang had so much fun playing with their new friends.
But before they knew it, it was time for Muno's family to go home.
Everyone was sad to say good-bye.

"It was nice to meet you," Foofa said.

"I hope you'll come back soon!" added Toodee.

"It's hard to say good-bye, but we had so much fun today!" said DJ Lance. "We met Muno's family and we learned the nice way to meet new people! Thanks for playing with us today! Good-bye!"

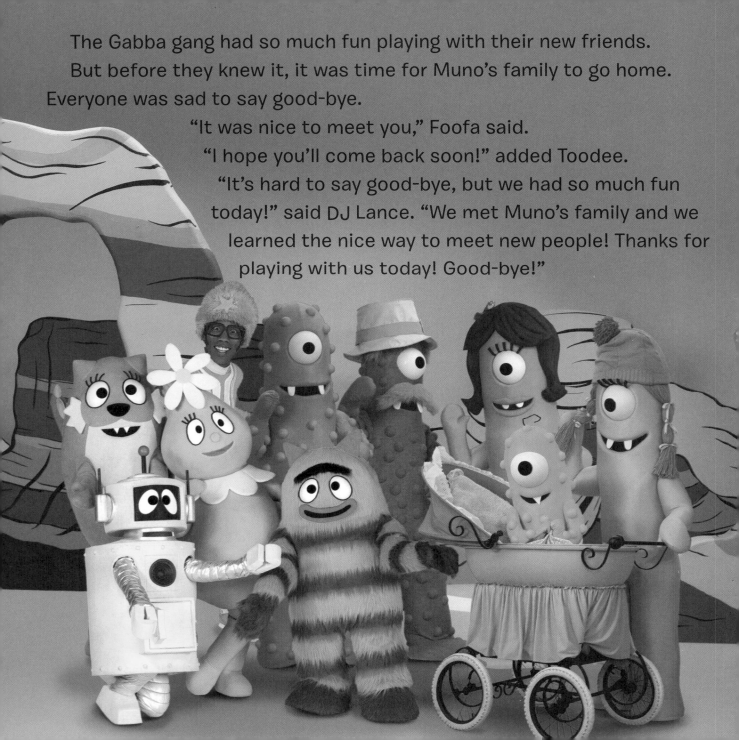